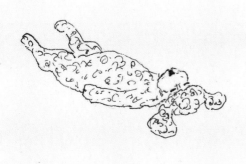

Published by Octobre Press
606 Azalea Lane, Vero Beach, Florida 32963

Book Design and Illustrations by Virginia Best
Editorial Development by Laura Ross
Art Editing by Cynthia Bardes
Assistant Art Editing by Amanda Robinson
Assistant Art Editing by David
PRINTED IN THE UNITED STATES

ISBN 978-1-7329768-0-1

Please visit the website for more information
www.PansythePoodle.com

Pansy in Rome
The Mystery of the Missing Cat

written by **Cynthia Bardes**   illustrations by **Virginia Best**

Pansy at the Palace
A Beverly Hills Mystery

written by Cynthia Bardes illustrations by Kim Weissenborn

Pansy in Africa
The Mystery of the Missing Lion Cub

written by Cynthia Bardes illustrations by Virginia Best

Pansy in Paris
A Mystery at the Museum

written by Cynthia Bardes illustrations by Virginia Best

Pansy in Venice
The Mystery of the Missing Parrot

written by Cynthia Bardes illustrations by Virginia Best

Pansy in London
The Mystery of the Missing Puppy

written by Cynthia Bardes illustrations by Virginia Best

Pansy in New York
The Mystery of the Missing Monkey

written by Cynthia Bardes illustrations by Virginia Best

Titles available in the Pansy the Poodle Mystery Series

Pansy toy dog

for Avery, Aubrey, Cindy, and David

Italia
(Italy)

ROMA
(ROME)

Many thanks to my good friends Ambassador and Mrs. Lewis M. Eisenberg for their hospitality at the Villa while I created Pansy's path around Rome.

Pasticceria

Torta + Cake

Biscotto + Cookie

Pasticcio + Pastry

I'm Pansy, the toy poodle and I love to go on adventures with my best friend Avery! Mama and Papa took us to Rome, Italy—and when we got there we were all very hungry.

Our first stop was the Trattoria Roma.

Trattoria means *restaurant* in Italian.

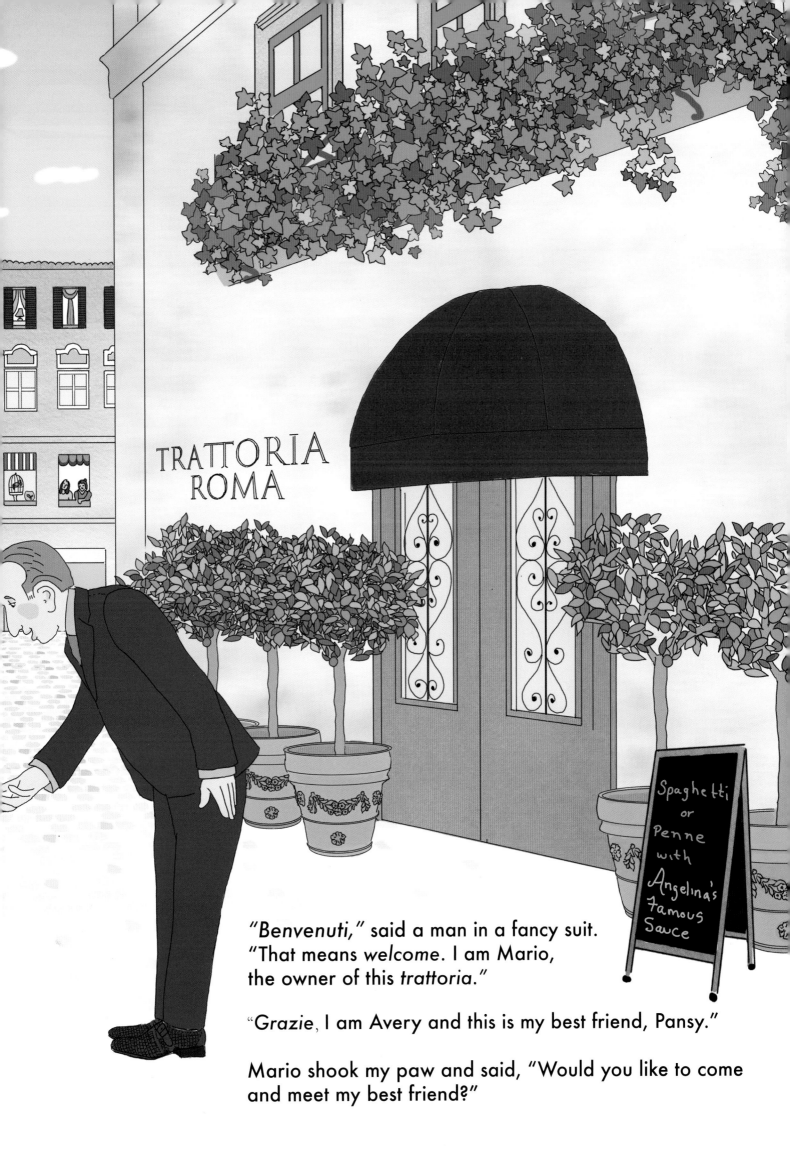

"*Benvenuti,*" said a man in a fancy suit.
"That means *welcome.* I am Mario,
the owner of this *trattoria.*"

"*Grazie,* I am Avery and this is my best friend, Pansy."

Mario shook my paw and said, "Would you like to come
and meet my best friend?"

We went through a swinging door and saw lots of people—and a big orange cat—all wearing tall white hats.

"These are my wonderful chefs," said Mario.

"Angelina," Mario said to the cat, "may I present Pansy and Avery?"

"Meow, meow, meow," said Angelina.

"Meow is Angelina's way of saying *ciao*," said Mario. "That means *hi*."

"*Ciao*," I said, but it came out, "A-wowww."

"We make the best spaghetti sauce in Rome,
and Angelina watches over it," said Mario. "When it is perfect,
she rings the little bell around her neck. She also peels garlic with her tiny claws."

"We can't wait to try your special sauce, Angelina!" said Avery.

"Avooo, avooo," I said. *It smells sooooo good!*

"Yum, yum," said Avery. "This is the best spaghetti sauce I've ever tasted!"

"Yip, yip, yip," I agreed. I slurped and slurped.

WHAM!
The kitchen doors BURST open!

"My Angelina! My Angelina!" screamed Mario. "She is gone! She would never go anywhere without me!"

Angelina's Special Sauce
* Spaghetti
* Linguine
* Fettuccine
* Penne
"the BEST sauce in ROME!"

"Oh, Signor Mario! We can help. Pansy is a famous detective but she needs clues."

"Hmmmm . . ." said Mario. "Angelina has blue eyes, wears a bell around her neck, and smells of garlic. She loves to play in Rome's many ruins. Angelina always meows three times in a row."

"Woof, woof, woof," I barked. So many good clues! Let's get started!

Sniff, sniff, sniff—I followed the scent of garlic all the way to a place that looked very old.

"This is a famous ruin called the Colosseum, Pansy," said Avery. "It is almost 2,000 years old! The Romans used to play games here. The players were called gladiators. Look, you can pretend to be a gladiator and play!"

I love to play! It would be fun to play hide-and-seek here! I jumped up and down.

"No time to play now, though," said Avery. "We have a job to do. Look at all the cats who live here!"

I saw cats, cats, and more cats—but no Angelina!

POPCORN
FLAVORS

Meatball
Cheese
Pistachio
Garlic

FANCY
POPCORN

I kept following my nose to a very busy open square called a piazza.
I could smell garlic to the left, to the right, and all around.

"Oh, Pansy," said Avery, "there are so many restaurants in Rome, and their chefs all cook with garlic. How will we ever find Angelina?"

I lay down and put my paws over my nose to think.

I saw something white on the ground—a tiny chef's hat just like Angelina's! "Woof, woof!" *This is a clue!*

Avery grabbed the hat and we kept running.

We came to another piazza. This one had a big fountain, and next to it a gray cat sat licking her paw.

"Awhooo," I said. *You are not Angelina.*

"Look, Pansy," said Avery. "The sign says 'Throw a coin in the fountain and make a wish.'"

I wished we could find Angelina.

Throw a coin in the Trevi Fountain and make a Wish ☆

Ding! Dong! Ding! Dong!
Avery and I heard a bell.
A bell *might* be a clue, I thought.

We raced through the narrow streets and up some wide, steep steps.
It was a church bell we heard, not Angelina's bell.

A priest standing outside the church waved and said, "*Buongiorno.*"

"*Buongiorno,* Father," said Avery. "Good day. We are looking for an orange cat with blue eyes and a bell around her neck."

"I saw a cat like that in the basket of Signor Antonio's Vespa scooter. He is the chef at Osteria Bella."

"Oh, no," said Avery looking at her map.
"That is very far away."

"I will take you on my Vespa," said the priest.
"Antonio makes my favorite gelato—pink
raspberry. *Gelato* is Italian ice cream
and it is very special."

"Awhooooooo!" I love ice cream!

"Hang on, Pansy!" yelled Avery.

"Yip, yip!" *This is fun!*

"See the dome across the Tiber River?" shouted the priest. "That is St. Peter's Basilica. *Basilica* is the word for a special church. It is in Vatican City, where the Pope lives and works."

"Buongiorno, Father," said Signor Antonio. "Will you and your friends be joining us for lunch?"

"Grazie, no," said Avery. "We are in a hurry to find a very special cat named Angelina."

"Meeeeooooow, meeeeooooow, MEEOOOOOOOOWWWWWWW."

My ears stood STRAIGHT UP!

When we pushed open the doors to the kitchen, there was Angelina! She was crying big cat tears—plop, plop, plop—into a bubbling pot of sauce.

Avery frowned at Antonio. "Why is Angelina here?"

Antonio looked at the floor. "I knew Angelina helped Mario make the best sauce in Rome. I wanted her to help me instead . . . but all she does is cry big, salty tears into the pot. My sauce is too salty now!"

"You must take Angelina home to Signor Mario and apologize right away!" said Avery.

"Grrrr, grrr, grr," I said.

"Meow, meow, MEEEOOOWW," Angelina sang all the way home.

"Awhooo," I howled to keep her company.

"Angelina, you're back!" cried Signor Mario, as she leapt into his arms. "Oh, Antonio, I thought we were friends. Why did you take my Angelina?"

"I just wanted my sauce to be as good as yours," Antonio said. "I am very sorry."

"It is wrong to take something that isn't yours, Signor Antonio," said Avery. "Instead of trying to copy Signor Mario, you must figure out what you do best."

"What can I do to make things right?" asked Antonio.

"I have an idea," said Mario.
"There are many hungry cats at the Colosseum.
You could make a big picnic to feed them—and
bring your delicious gelato for dessert!"

"I will do it!" said Antonio. "I will make special
liver gelato and fish pizza just for them!"

"We will help because good friends
always help each other," said Mario.
Angelina purred and purred in Mario's arms.

I leapt and twirled and Avery clapped her hands. We love picnics!

On Sunday, we all went to the Colosseum. The picnic was wonderful!
The cats ate and ate and so did Avery and I.

When we were all full and happy, Mario said, "Pansy and Avery, as a reward for your good deeds, I'd like to take you to one of my favorite places."

He took us to some beautiful gardens where we went on a boat ride around a little lake.

"I love Rome," said Avery, "and I love sharing it with my best friend!"

"Yip, yip!" I said. That's me!